this
Oriel Book
belongs to

LAURA'S GIFT

LAURA'S GIFT

DEE JACOBS

Illustrations by Kris Karlsson

ORIEL
PRESS

ISBN 0-938628-00-3

Cover Design by Chas. S. Politz/Design Council, Inc.

Jacobs, Dee, 1934-
    Laura's Gift

ISBN 0-938628-00-3

I. Title

PS8569.A288L38   C813'.5'4   C79-090045-9
PR9199.3.J33L38

To Mort —
who is responsible for all commas
and much, much more . . .

It was her favorite time in the whole day. She snuggled into her pillow and eased herself into the warmth of her old comforter, pulling it up around her ears. There was still a morning chill in the air, but the sun was already breaking through the uncurtained windows. The clump of birches outside her window was bursting into a coat of fresh green. She turned from her side to her back and her eyes skirted the molding of the high ceiling, following a crack. Her gaze stopped on what she considered one of the room's most distinctive features. Three peacock feathers with turquoise eyes were affixed, seemingly randomly, to the ceiling's plaster. Peacock feathers she and Laura had found at the zoo. They had been lucky enough to go on a day when the birds were shedding their old tails for new. She and Laura had used them for book-marks until the day when what promised to be an unfortunate accident turned into quite a happy one.

Her mind wandered back to that day. It was one she would not forget. Her mother had bought them a hanging-basket chair. She and Laura were delighted, and so was her mother because it had been a bargain. Her father was not so delighted because he really wasn't very good at fixing or hanging things, and he freely admitted it. Her mother prevailed upon him, and he did his best.

He explained to Laura and Catherine that to hang a hanging-basket chair a hook must first be screwed into a beam. He told them that the way to find a beam was to knock on the ceiling until you heard a solid sound which was a very different kind of a sound from the empty sound you heard when you were not hitting a beam.

After he did a lot of knocking on the ceiling with a broom handle he marked a place on the ceiling with a pencil, carried a drill up the ladder and drilled a very large hole where the large hook was to be inserted. It was to the large hook you attached the hanging-basket chair. Quite a bit of plaster fell on him and he announced that he had not found a beam. Three very large holes and quite a bit of fallen plaster later, he found a beam. Getting the hook in after that was comparatively simple except that as he was screwing the hook in he gave his thumb a purple blood-blister which he nursed for a week or two.

She and Laura loved that hanging-basket chair. It hung parallel to the wide window and they could propel each other, while swinging in it, the entire width of the room. It was as good as having a playground in your own bedroom. The gaping holes left by the three mistakes they covered with those peacock feathers, which they taped to the good parts of the plaster left around them.

Her mother and father agreed. The ceiling was much prettier with the peacock feathers than without them.

The room was large and functional. There was ample walking space around each of the twin beds. The wall against which the headboards of the beds were placed had built-in bookshelves up to the ceiling. There was a desk against the wall opposite the hanging-basket chair. The wall closest to the hanging-basket chair the girls had covered with posters. The hardwood floor was bare of rugs but was clean and gleaming.

Catherine loved that room.

She knew that in a very short time she would hear her mother come down the stairs and that her mother would be humming as she filled the coffee-pot and put the bacon on to fry.

Every morning was like that. The same delicious sounds and aromas. That was because her mother said she had many vices, but if she had to give up any of them, the last would be the first cup of coffee in the morning and bacon for breakfast.

And she knew that as soon as Laura heard her mother in the kitchen, Laura would open her eyes. Eyes very much like her own: open and blue, but kinder. She knew that as soon as Laura's gaze met hers it would be time to leave the warmth of her bed, face the still chill of the morning, scramble into navy-blue tights, a white wash-and-wear shirt, a navy-blue tie, and throw over her head a navy-blue tunic. The last thing she would scramble into, and then not until it was time to leave, would be a pair of hideous black oxfords that only old ladies wore.

"Good morning, my chickadees," said her mother, as she and Laura sat down to breakfast. "Catherine, you are not looking particularly spirited this morning."

"It is difficult to feel spirited on a Monday morning when you have to face the prospect of a whole week of going to the esteemed St. Hilda's School for Girls, and worse, to look at the face of the esteemed Miss Vertue every morning for five days in a row, and worse yet, to listen to her lecture for one hour every morning on the horrors of the dangling participle!" She exchanged an amused glance with Laura. That was their private joke.

"You don't make it sound particularly appealing," her mother said, "but I don't think I would allow it to sour my whole day."

"It's not only that, Mumzie dear. As you know, it is on Mondays, no matter how inclement the weather, it is the duty of St. Hilda's girls

2

to entertain the high-school kids across the street on their lunch break, by stripping ourselves of our stunning tunics, donning white shorts, and treating them to the spectacle of a rousing game of field-hockey. Speaking of which, where is our resident athlete?"

"If you mean your brother Jeff, the baseball coach is treating all the little kids on the team to breakfast before school."

"How disgusting! Mother, after you and Dad had two such lovely children as Laura and myself, how did you manage to produce a creature like him?"

Laura looked at her mother. "Cath, you really are much too hard on Jeff. He really is an O.K. kid."

"Laura is right, Catherine. You are old enough to exercise much more patience with him than you do."

"He's beastly." Catherine was definite.

"Catherine, when you were nine, you were not so terribly elegant yourself. Please try and remember that. Now if you girls do not want to earn more demerit points for your class, you'd best prepare yourselves to leave. It's getting late."

"Is Dad taking us to school today?" asked Laura.

"No, dear, he had a lot of papers to correct, so he left for the college very early. He said it would be easier to grab a bit of breakfast in the faculty dining room after his first class, so he left the van. I'll drive you. Now hurry and brush your teeth. Catherine, do you know where you left your shoes?"

Laura and her mother waited for her while she made a mad dash through the house. She finally found the shoes under the piano where she had kicked them off the night before.

She plunked herself breathless into the van.

"Catherine, it amazes me you can be so intolerant of Jeffrey. Your own habits leave something to be desired. You know of course that your holding us up like this has caused both you and your sister to be late for school again. And I am getting a little tired of those notes from Miss Vertue, addressing herself to the subject of your tardiness."

"Well, I for one," said Catherine, "would be happy if she carried out her threats of expulsion. And you know perfectly well she never would."

Her mother shot her a sidelong glance. "Catherine, in the first place it is not just 'you-for-one'. Your sister becomes a victim of your thoughtlessness. She's incriminated along with you and through no doing of hers. In the second place, I asked you to get a fresh wash-rag and sponge those spots of maple syrup off the front of your tunic. I can see very clearly that you did not. And in the third place, you are wearing that worn-out old forest-green cardigan again. You know it's not regulation."

"I couldn't find the navy-blue one and I happen to be very fond of this old sweater."

"Not getting off to a very good start this morning, are we, Catherine? I hope when you return this afternoon things will be better."

Catherine did not answer her mother but concentrated on looking out the window. They passed the junior high school they would have been going to if they were not going to St. Hilda's. The reason her parents gave the girls for sending them to private school was that it was academically superior, and that the girls were fortunate their grades were good, because their father being a professor, they could attend at a substantially reduced tuition. But Catherine knew the real reason was that there were sixteen steps leading up to the front door of that public school and twelve steps leading up to the three side doors. And that after you got into the landing there were eight more steps leading up to the main floor and more steps up to the second floor and more steps down to the basement where the shop and home-ec classes were held. St. Hilda's was a one-story building with only three steps leading into all the doors. The halls were long but there were no stairs at all. She decided that for Laura's sake she must try harder to like St. Hilda's.

The school ground was empty as her mother pulled the van up to the front door.

"I'm sorry I made you late again, Laura."

Laura grinned and shrugged casually. Catherine knew her sister did not care any more about being late than she.

"Mother," said Catherine, "I'm sorry, and I really will try harder to be nice today. Mom, you don't need to get out. Laura and I can manage the stairs without you."

And her mother knew they could. She waved good-bye and blew them a kiss as she drove off.

"I'm afraid I've really got us into hot water, Laura. Miss Vertue is always such a crab Monday mornings."

"Maybe that's because she spends the week-ends alone," mused Laura as they sped down the hall to the door marked 8A. "Anyway, don't worry about it. We've heard Miss Vertue rave before today."

The class of 8A was lined up against the wall as Laura and Catherine burst in the door. Miss Vertue looked as though she were the queen inspecting the guard. She walked sedately down the line, and as she passed each girl her head, with its severe bun, gave a slight nod. The rhythm of her inspection was broken on the entrance of the two girls.

Her eyes narrowed visibly as she said in a voice that would freeze a desert rat, "I see the Devon girls are late again." She addressed the line as she continued: "Girls, do you suppose it is because the Devon household cannot afford a clock?"

There was tittering down the line. The expression on Laura's and Catherine's faces mirrored each other's. The sisters were 'scholarship' students in a school where it was a common sight, at the end of the school day, to see chauffeur-driven limousines picking up their charges as they emptied out of the academy. Miss Vertue's remark was cruel.

"Miss Catherine Devon and Miss Laura Devon, would you stand at the end of the line and I will finish inspection."

As she approached Laura she remarked sarcastically that at least one of the Devon girls took pride in her appearance. "Catherine, it seems not only that you cannot afford a clock, but you also cannot afford a comb." Catherine's hair was cropped short and such a mass of curls it could never give the appearance of being tidy. "You persist in wearing that non-regulation cardigan, and from the front of your tunic I can tell the class what you had for breakfast this morning. Your stockings have a run in them from the knee to the toe (Catherine had suffered that mishap when helping Laura out of the van), and I don't believe your oxfords have seen a can of polish for one month. You have outdone yourself this morning, and for the class your appearance has earned ten demerit points. And since you seem unable to grasp the fact that a St. Hilda's girl wears *only* a St. Hilda's uniform, I shall warn you that if you appear in class one more time wearing *any* non-regulation cardigan, I will take more serious measures . . . . Now, class, return to your seats and we will commence our study of the English language."

There was a soft groan as Miss Vertue walked to the blackboard. As principal of the school, out of devotion to grammar she had over the past ten years given the first hour of the teaching day to the class of graduating girls. This class was no different from the ones that had gone before. They did not appreciate her sacrifice.

She picked up a piece of chalk and in a precise hand wrote, "A St. Hilda's girl shall always be true." She placed the chalk tidily on the ledge under the board and as she turned around to face the class she rubbed her hands together to remove the last traces of chalk-dust.

"Now we will analyze the sentence. First we will quickly run through the parts of speech. Then we will discuss, briefly, meaning. You will then write a two-page paper using the sentence as the paper's title. Catherine, you may begin by parsing the sentence for us. Please identify the modal auxiliary 'shall'."

Catherine correctly saw 'St. Hilda's' as a single part of the sentence, that is as a noun in the possessive case. Her ears still felt hot from the remark Miss Vertue had made about the clock. She took a deep breath: "I would be happy to continue, Miss Vertue, but I would

prefer to do a different sentence."

"And may I ask why?"

Miss Vertue's neck was beginning to turn red.

"Miss Vertue, I think the sentence is a little old-fashioned. No one uses 'shall' any more to express an order. And I don't think you can order even a St. Hilda's girl to be 'true'. To be true is something you *choose* to be."

Miss Vertue's nose always ran when she was upset, and her nose was running now. She now went to the same place she always went to when she was looking for a handkerchief. Her hand disappeared behind the high-buttoned flounce of her blouse; down into the depths of her bosom, which was set very low. That was Laura's and Catherine's private joke; Miss Dangling Participle, they called her. It was a process the class of 8A found most fascinating. They always wondered if the frantic race would be won by the drop rapidly forming on the end of her nose, or if her hand would reach the handkerchief in time to catch the drop. Laura and Catherine had kept score. So far, her hand and the handkerchief always won.

She wiped her nose, and by now the red in her neck had spread up to her forehead. "Catherine Devon, you are impertinent. Born as twins, I am at a loss to understand how you could be so different from your sister."

Catherine knew she was already in deep trouble but she went on, "Miss Vertue, I believe you just constructed a sentence using a dangling participle."

The room was as quiet as ever it was when vacated on a hot day in July. Even the girls who had never earned a demerit point were frightened. Miss Vertue drew herself so taut she looked as though her head was being pulled up to the ceiling by a string. Her eyes watered as she fixed them on Catherine: "I will discuss this matter with you when school is over. Your behavior is something I cannot put up with."

Catherine wanted to tell her she had just succeeded in ending a sentence with a preposition but this time she bit her tongue. Even Catherine was beginning to sense her own impertinence, and a strange feeling of remorse came over her as she realized that in her attempt to save face, she had hurt Miss Vertue. She had not wanted to do that. She took herself through the rest of the hour in a daze, and even when Miss Robinson, the math teacher, came in for the next period, Catherine, who usually enjoyed math and Miss Robinson, could not concentrate. She kept wishing the day would be over.

Third period was field-hockey. Laura went to a little room adjacent to the office. In the little room was a narrow cot. Off the room was another one with a toilet and a sink. Laura rested third period. She could not play field-hockey from a wheel-chair.

II

L unch at St. Hilda's was a formal affair. The food was definitely
institutional: plain and bland with a heavy emphasis on mashed
potatoes and pale gravy. The salads generally ran to either red jello
with bananas, or green jello with lumps of canned pineapple. They
were invariably so gummy a fork sprang off them like a rubber ball
bouncing against a wall, or so liquid the only possible way to trans-
port the arrangement to your mouth was with a spoon. Yes, the food
was most certainly uninteresting, but the table-settings were something else. Fresh white linen table-cloths dressed each rectangular
table. The service was silver, and each place-setting was complete
with salad fork and soup spoon. If a St. Hilda's girl, upon entering,
did not know that she was to use the utensils as she progressed
through the meal from the outside to the inside, she soon learned. The
plates were white (though that did not enhance the appearance of the
colorless food as it lay upon them) but of bone china. The glasses were
not crystal (breakage would have been too high) but clear glasses
sitting at each place shone spotlessly. The tables wore seasonal center-
pieces, usually of flowers picked from the gardens of St. Hilda's, and
arranged by the girls taking home economics.

There were fourteen tables in the dining room and twelve girls sat at
each table. Five sat at each side, and one girl sat at each end. The girls
sitting at the end of the table were the older ones, the seventh and
eighth graders.

The routine at lunch was structured. The girls filed in and took their
assigned seats. On the first Monday of each month the girls were
reassigned to a different table. Before they sat down to eat, they stood
behind their chairs and sang:

> Praise God from whom all blessings flow;
> Praise Him, all creatures here below;
> Praise Him above ye heavenly host;
> Praise Father, Son and Holy Ghost.

(Catherine loved the long 'Amen'.)

Then the girl assigned to the north end of the table would nod for
everyone to sit down. When they were seated she would go to the
buffet at the end of the long room and bring a tray prepared with
twelve salads. She would place them at her end of the table and serve.

When the first course was finished, the girl at the south end of the table would remove the dishes as the first girl returned with the second course.

Lunch at St. Hilda's took sixty minutes. One of the teachers was always there to supervise. If an unwary girl was caught spread-eagling her arms as she cut her meat, which was always tough, the supervisor took from the end of the buffet two thin books which she placed under the offender's arm-pits. The offender was then obliged to wield her knife, fork, and spoon for the duration of the meal while holding the books to her sides.

Laura and Catherine were not sitting at the same table that day, and because Laura's schedule in the afternoons was different from her own, Catherine whispered hurriedly to Laura as the lunch-line was forming, "Tell Mom, when she comes to pick us up, that I have some extra stuff to do after school and not to wait. I'll walk home when I'm through."

The afternoon dragged on for Catherine. She became more and more apprehensive as her meeting with Miss Vertue approached.

✳ ✳ ✳ ✳ ✳

The meeting did not go at all as Catherine had suspected. In fact, the course of that meeting was so different that, as she walked home, she was absorbed in thought. For Catherine had strong opinions on just about everything and most especially, people. It had not occurred to her that her opinions about them could be wrong; not until Miss Vertue had talked to her after school that day. Miss Vertue had taken her completely by surprise.

She hurried up the walk, anxious to greet Laura.

"How did it go, Cath?" asked Laura from her position on the hard-backed chair that sat in the living-room beside the piano.

"I'll tell you about it after supper. Where's Mom?"

"She went to get her hair cut. Are you going to tell Mom and Dad?"

"I'll tell them what I have to, at supper-time. Did Mom leave us any treats?"

"Yes, Catherine," said Laura, realizing she was not going to get any information about the meeting with Miss Vertue until Catherine was ready. Laura understood her sister very well. "She left cheese and fruit and a special treat—three bags of M & M's— one for each of us."

"Where's Jeffrey?"

"He's still at baseball practice. You'd better get started on your own. It's getting late."

"Laura, I don't feel like practising this afternoon. It's been such a terrible day."

"Catherine, your piano exam is only two months away, and if you want to win another music scholarship, you don't have any time to waste. And your lesson is tomorrow."

"Scales, scales, all Ms. Freeman wants to hear are scales. I hate them."

Laura rose slowly, and with a gait peculiar to those wearing leg braces, covered the distance from her chair to the lid of the piano. It was a grand piano and almost dwarfed the living-room, which was not grand. She picked from the lid's surface a dictation book and as she returned slowly, painstakingly, to the hard-backed chair, she leafed through the book until she got to the last entry.

"Here they are, Catherine. A list of scales that will be required of you on your exam."

"I know, Laura, and the first scale on the list is C major. You'd think C major would be the easiest because it doesn't have any black keys. But it's the hardest. Ms. Freeman gets me on it every time."

"I have an idea, Catherine," said Laura as she again rose slowly from her chair. She approached the coffee table with hesitation in her step but determination on her face. She picked up Catherine's bag of M & M's, opened them and spilled them on the table. "Count them, Catherine."

"For heaven's sake, why?"

"Just count them."

So Catherine did. "There are forty-four," she announced after a quick count.

"O.K. Put them back in the bag and give them to me when I'm back in that chair beside the piano," commanded Laura.

Catherine could not imagine what Laura was up to, and by now was eager to find out.

"There are eighteen scales listed here in your dictation book. Nine major scales and nine related minor scales. I'll call them out to you, and every time you succeed in playing a scale correctly three times in a row, I'll pop two M & M's into your mouth. When you've done all eighteen of them, there will still be eight M & M's left. Those you can put in your mouth all at once as your reward for doing such a good job."

"I don't see how that is going to help me play scales, but it's worth a try."

Catherine spent more time on scales than she ever had in her life. Never had she enjoyed it so much. Nor did she have to be encouraged to practise her pieces. She loved music and enjoyed the challenge of learning new things. Laura shared her love. Laura had a fine contralto voice, and sometimes as she read and Catherine played, she would hum with Catherine's melody the contralto line. Catherine enjoyed it when Laura did that, for it helped her hear the distinct voices.

"That was a good practice, Laura. Thanks. I hear Mom in the kitchen. She must have come in the back door. You rest now and I'll go help her."

It was an hour Catherine looked forward to. It was the one hour in the day she could be alone with her mother. They always had a good visit; her mother could sense her mood and respond to it.

"Sounded like a good practice, Cath."

"Hmmmm," said Catherine absently.

"Well, how will we dress the chops tonight?" her mother queried.

There was no response. Ordinarily the question itself would have evoked at least a chuckle.

"That's what I don't like about cooking," her mother continued, "you never get a dress-rehearsal before the final performance."

No response. Her mother determined something must have happened at school, and that day she might as well not try to make jokes.

"Catherine, I think I'll use up those apples in the crisper to make applesauce. I'll peel and you can chop. I'll serve it along with the chops, which I'll bake in that tomato sauce Laura is so fond of."

Mrs. Devon was not particularly fond of cooking. It was the loneliness of it she did not like. Her worries and concerns seemed to weigh more heavily at dusk: just the time supper preparations had to be undertaken. Still, she knew how important it was for Laura to eat well, so she was a conscientious cook and made a special effort to fix meals Laura liked. It was fun visiting with Catherine, and she was grateful to her for both the help and the company she afforded. Even when she was not in a jolly mood, it was still good to have her there. Catherine was particularly good company when she was in one of her rather reflective moods, and some of their best talks came then. And it was not unusual, on an ordinary day, for Catherine to turn on the radio, find a jazzy tune, and get her mother dancing a toe-tapping number as Catherine wielded something like a celery stick as a baton.

Mrs. Devon knew this would not be one of those nights. That was all right. Mrs. Devon had some preoccupations of her own.

※ ※ ※ ※ ※

The Devon family sat in the dining-room for supper.

"I'm taking you to the symphony tonight, Josie."

"You are? What a surprise!"

"Yes, and you'd better look fancy tonight, Josephine." Switching from pet names was a sign of mock-seriousness in the Devon household chatter.

"Why is that, Peter?" she asked laughingly.

"Because we're sitting in fancy seats!"

"Well in that case, I'll do my best. Lucky I got my hair cut this afternoon!"

"Too bad you didn't take Jeff with you," snapped Catherine; "he looks like a water-buffalo."

Jeff responded by cutting more fiercely into his chop.

Catherine continued, "I don't know why we have to eat with him .... Look at him! He holds his fork like a Cro-Magnon man. And why does he always have to wear that stupid baseball cap?"

"You know, Kate," said her father, "your tongue is doing more to spoil this supper for us than either Jeffrey's appearance or his table-manners. And Jeff might respond to you if you would refer to him in something other than the third person. But his strategy of paying no attention to you at all is working very nicely. Jeff provokes you by his silence as much as you undoubtedly provoke him with your remarks. In fact, I think Jeff has the edge in this contest."

"All right," Catherine sighed, "Jeff, my dear, dear little brother, would you please take off your cap?"

Jeffrey surprised everyone at the table by obliging. Catherine decided now would be as good a time as any to tell her parents about what she had to do on Saturday morning. "Oh, after Laura's therapy Saturday morning, don't come back to the house for me. I'll just meet you at the library at one o'clock, Laura." Catherine tried to sound casual.

"And what are your plans for Saturday morning, Catherine?" asked her mother, who knew something was in the wind.

"They aren't my plans, Mom. They're Miss Vertue's plans. One of the kitchen staff is down sick, and Miss Vertue has assigned me the task of helping with polishing the silver."

Laura thought of all those tables and all that silver. "Oh Catherine, so many knives, forks, and spoons!"

"I know," Catherine said glumly.

"Let's hear it, Kate," said her dad, "what did you do this time? Miss Vertue had to have a reason for assigning you such a chore."

"Well, I lost my shoes this morning before school, which made Laura and me late again. Then Miss Vertue was not pleased with my appearance and gave the class ten demerit points. Then she was not pleased with me during the grammar lesson, and since I guess she was tired of giving the class demerit points I had earned, she decided polishing silver would help build my character, something I gather she feels I need to improve."

Laura wondered why her sister had given such scanty details. Her mother and dad knew that Catherine's details were scanty, but they did not press the issue. They knew that Catherine would tell them what really happened when she was ready to.

"What are demerit points?" asked Jeff.

"It's a barbaric system, Jeff, where the sins of a few are visited upon the many," replied Catherine.

"I'll explain it to you, Jeff," said Laura. "At St. Hilda's we have a plaque. The plaque is the crest of St. Hilda's."

"Like the one you have sewn on the pocket of your tunic?"

"Yes, Jeff, just like that, only it is enameled and mounted on a crest-shaped piece of walnut." Laura continued, "Every morning in every class we have inspection. If there is something wrong with our uniform, we earn a demerit point. If we comb our hair in class, we earn a demerit point. If we chew gum, we do, too. It's ridiculous, lots of things like that. At the end of each week the teacher tallies the score. The class earning the fewest demerit points gets to have the plaque hanging in their classroom the following week."

"How many times has 8A won the plaque this year?" asked Jeff.

"Not once," replied Catherine, "and it's killing Miss Vertue because we are the graduating class, and are supposed to be setting an example. I think it's a stupid idea. If you win the plaque it's not something you won for yourself. If you lose, everyone in the class is down on you because it's your fault. Most everyone in that class is down on me most of the time. But I don't care whether a plaque hangs in our class or it doesn't," Catherine stated matter-of-factly.

"Well, if I were you *I'd* want to win the plaque!" exclaimed Jeff.

"That's because you're team-spirited," Catherine sneered, "and the reason you're team-spirited is because you can't function without somebody else."

"I don't think anyone can function alone," Mrs. Devon interjected, "I mean not completely alone."

"That's true and it isn't true, Mother," Laura broke in. "I'm sociable because I love people and need their company. I'm alone, too, because we are all alone . . . . I mean, who I am depends on the choices I make, and no one can make those choices for me; so we *are* all alone."

The Devons continued supper quietly; Jeff, chomping away, was the happy exception. Catherine envied him just a little . . . .

III

Catherine felt the excitement in the air. She knew her mother and Laura felt it too. She stood at the head of the stairs as she watched her father bow, sweep Laura out of her wheel-chair, and announce with mock dignity, "Come, my princess, you and your sister may watch your mother, the queen, prepare herself for the concert. The symphony is performing tonight, in her honor!"

Catherine watched Laura wrap her arms around her father's neck and saw the anticipation on her face as she took her royal ride to her parents' bedroom. Mr. and Mrs. Devon went out rarely of an evening, and when they did, it was an occasion.

Mr. Devon placed Laura on the big bed, propping her comfortably with pillows. Then Catherine, Laura, and Mrs. Devon settled into the game they played on nights like this one.

Josephine Devon enjoyed playing the game as much as the girls. Her days were full, and the extra duties required of her because of Laura's handicap left her little time to concern herself with fashion. She was a tidy and attractive woman, but her everyday wardrobe steered itself always in the direction of practicality. Getting dressed up was fun for her too.

"Well, girls, who should I be tonight?" She stepped into the commodious closet.

"I've been reading the poems of Emily Dickinson. Did you know that for the last twenty-four years of her life she only wore white?" Laura continued, "Mom, you could wear your white lace dress and go as Emily Dickinson."

"Hardly anyone but you would know that, Laura," answered Catherine, "so if Mom went as Emily Dickinson she might as well go as Sara Lee, who isn't even a real person. No one would know who she was supposed to be. Besides, it's still too cold to wear white."

"Cath's right about the color, Laura. So where do we go from here?"

"I know," announced Catherine, "don't go as anyone in particular. Go as the queen of the gypsies! You could wear that long, tiered paisley. The one with the full sleeves and the peasant neck. Wear the red shawl with the six-inch fringe. Laura and I will deck you out in gypsy jewels."

"Good idea! Does it meet with your approval, Laura?"

Catherine was already on her way to her mother's jewel-box as Laura nodded her approval. She opened the second drawer of her mother's dresser and lifted from it a large black leather box. The leather was soft and supple to the touch. The box itself was fitted with shiny gold hardware. It had a place for a key but was never locked. Mrs. Devon kept the key inside the box. The inside of the box was glorious. It was upholstered in the softest red velvet Catherine had ever touched.

The jewel-box had two layers. The top layer rested on a rim that described the perimeter of the box midway around its depth. That layer lifted out to reveal a second layer and its treasures, underneath. Each layer was partitioned differently, allowing spaces for rings, earrings, lockets, chains, and crystal beads. Catherine and Laura loved going through it. Their mother had many beautiful jewels that had been passed on to her through her side of the family. Her family was from England, and, as far as her mother knew, all of them were dead. The last one to die had been Josephine Devon's great-aunt Kitty, after whom Catherine had been named.

Contained within the jewel-box was another much smaller one. That box was Catherine's and Laura's, and had been given them by that same 'Auntie Kitty'. In the small box was a piece of thin stationery which had been folded and re-folded many times. For each time the girls explored their mother's jewel-box, they explored their own. The note read:

> Dearest Josephine,
> My dear. Didn't you surprise us all? Not one but two beautiful baby girls! I was so hoping for a girl but never could have imagined I'd be so pleasantly surprised. I wanted to give your new baby something of mine. Something very special to me. I had selected a gift, but now I have changed my mind. I think this gift especially appropriate for your twin girls, Laura and Catherine. Especially appropriate because the stones in these pins are garnets, for January, the month of their birth, and although they are matching pins, each stone is unique.
> Please give them to Laura and Catherine on my behalf, when they are old enough to enjoy them.
> Lovingly,
> Aunt Katherine

Inside that small box and pinned to the satin lining were two small but exquisite heart-shaped pins. Pearls framed the edges, and in the center of each was set in gold a deep ruby garnet. Laura and Catherine prized them.

"What baubles have you girls picked out for me?"

Laura handed her mother some large gold hoops. "I think a gypsy queen would wear these."

"I think you're right, Laura. I don't think she'd go anywhere without them!"

"Wear rings, Mom. At least two on each hand. Here, wear the jade one and the pearl one on this hand, the turquoise and the topaz on the other."

Mrs. Devon laughed as Catherine slipped them on her fingers.

"This will finish you," Laura said as she passed a set of gold bangle-bracelets to Catherine, who passed them on to her mother. "Oh, you *do* look beautiful!"

Catherine noticed that the tired lines which usually appeared around her mother's eyes around supper-time had disappeared. Tonight, her brown eyes were dancing and there was a flush to her cheeks. With her fair skin and dark sleek hair, she could have been a gypsy queen, Catherine thought. Catherine also thought her mother extraordinarily pretty.

Mrs. Devon *felt* beautiful as she hugged her children.

✳ ✳ ✳ ✳ ✳

"Good night, kids. Your mother and I will not be late, but we'll expect you to be asleep by the time we get home. Jeff, I'll check your spelling in the morning. Laura and Catherine, when you go to bed don't talk too long. You both need your beauty sleep!"

"Yes Dad, so we can look good for Miss Vertue!" joked Catherine.

In the excitement Catherine had forgotten about her strange interview with Miss Vertue. Now, as she pushed Laura in the hanging-basket chair, she had to tell her about it. "It was weird, Laura. I expected Miss Vertue would be breathing fire. But when I went into her office she was very quiet. She seemed sad . . . . Laura, as I push you, work on your left leg. See if you can raise it with the momentum of the swing."

The hanging-basket chair exercise routine was an invention of the girls. Catherine pushed the swing, and with each forward thrust Laura worked on raising each leg alternately. Then she worked at raising them together. They would do this until Laura grew tired. Then she rested as Catherine continued to push. It was a freeing time for Laura. Swinging free in that hanging-basket chair allowed her to forget her handicap. As the swing lifted the girl she could even imagine what it must feel like to fly.

It was a nighly ritual Catherine enjoyed too. Like their mother, Laura was a good listener. Catherine continued, "I stood there facing Miss Vertue, and she asked me to sit down. She'd never invited me to sit down before! Then you'll never guess what she did, Laura. She apologized! She told me she regretted having made the remark about the clock . . . , that perhaps we could not afford one. She said that occasionally her tongue got ahead of her brain, but that it was a habit she had, for the most part, learned to control. Then she told me it was a bad habit I had, too, and one I indulged in far too often. Then she started acting like the same old Miss Vertue again. She told me that if I were punished, perhaps the next time I would think before I spoke. That's when she gave me the job of polishing silver. When I was leaving, she told me that this time she would not take the matter of my impertinence to Mom and Dad."

"That was nice of her, Catherine. Mom and Dad would not have liked to know how snippy you were."

"I know. I was really relieved . . . . I'll help you buckle your night-braces, Laura. We'd better get to bed."

Laura slept in special soft braces at night to help keep the muscles in her legs from contracting.

Catherine lay in bed thinking better thoughts about the evening. "Didn't Mom look nice tonight?"

"Yes. Yes, she did. Maybe she could go as Emily Dickinson next time," mused Laura.

"I suppose she could. It wouldn't really matter if no one knew who she was supposed to be."

"I checked a book of Emily Dickinson's poetry out of the library. Her poetry is gorgeous. I read a good one this afternoon. It really goes with this time of year. Let me read it to you."

"Save it for tomorrow, Laura. I want to go to sleep."

Laura had already switched on the lamp that rested on the night table beside her bed. "Oh, Cath, it's not very long. It will only take a minute. It's called, 'The Saddest Noise, The Sweetest Noise.' " She began reading softly:

The saddest noise, the sweetest noise,
The maddest noise that grows,
The birds, they make it in the spring,
At night's delicious close.

Between the March and April line,
That magical frontier
Beyond which summer hesitates,
Almost too heavenly near.

It makes us think of all the dead
That sauntered with us here,
By separation's sorcery
Made cruelly more dear.

It makes us think of what we had,
And what we now deplore
We almost wish those siren throats
Would go, and sing no more.

An ear can break a human heart
As quickly as a spear;
We wish the ear had not a heart
So dangerously near.

Catherine didn't know why, but an uneasy feeling always came over her when Laura read poems to her. For Laura's choices touched in her a chord she did not wish to hear. But she responded to Laura's reading honestly enough: "It's a beautiful poem. I especially liked the last two lines about your ear and your heart being so close together. Like when you listen to music you feel something that is not even musical. But I'd never thought of it that way before."

"Neither had I. Why is it that the bird's evening song in the spring does seem to sound sweeter than it does in the summer?"

"I think it's probably because we haven't heard them sing all winter. We just notice the song more in the spring," answered Catherine.

"I do think it is a sad song . . . , the birds singing at night. It makes me remember when . . . ." Laura broke off.

"It makes you remember what, Laura?"

"Oh, never mind," Laura answered distantly.

"That's what gets me about you, Laura. Sometimes you get started on a subject and you won't finish. It's like you had a secret and you won't share!"

"Nonsense, Cath. I was just going to say I get a lonely feeling . . . , that's all."

Catherine still felt Laura was withholding something, but decided to let it go. "Laura, turn off the light. Let's go to sleep, I'm tired."

That was the end of the discussion. Laura switched off the light and felt relieved to lie down, for she was tired too. After a moment she said, "Catherine, I want you to have Auntie Kitty's pin."

"I *do* have Auntie Kitty's pin."

"No, I mean I want you to have mine, Cath."

Catherine sometimes really didn't wish to understand her sister. Catherine yawned, "Please go to sleep, Laura."

"All right . . . , but remember, Catherine."

"Ummmmmm . . . ." Catherine did not answer, but had a thought or two that kept her from going to sleep immediately. She could see the outline of her sister's form in the bed across from her. She wondered why it had to be Laura.

And sleep overtook her.

IV

The exterior of the library was not commanding. It was a square old building, built with sandstone blocks dug from the local quarry. The architect, long since dead—the year of its completion was inscribed on the top of the square arch which framed the wide doors: 1907—had attempted to lend some degree of grandeur to the ugly box by fronting its face with marble stairs running the entire width of the entrance. The stairs were flanked by wide balustrades, at the bottom of which, and on each side, sat two camels. Catherine studied them as she waited for her father to deliver Laura. She decided those camels were ugly. She wondered why such a stupid animal had been chosen to stand silent guard over the portals of a library. She decided lions would have been a much better choice.

She watched her father drive up to the library's entrance. The hydraulically operated door of the van opened. The lift carrying Laura in her wheel-chair eased her to curb level. Her father released the safety catch which secured the chair to the lift.

"Thanks, Dad," Laura said as she propelled herself over to Catherine. "We'll be home in a couple of hours. It's a nice day. We'll walk. Hi. Have you been waiting long?"

"No, I just got here. Come on, let's go in."

Mounting the steps presented no problem. Dividing them midway across were two sturdy iron railings. These enclosed a ramp which ran from the street up to the landing. At the end of the ramp, imbedded in the sandstone face of the building, was a small, narrow brass plaque. Inscribed on the plaque were the words:

THIS RAMP DONATED TO THE HANDICAPPED
BY THE LIONS CLUB 1970

The girls hurried past the check-out desk and approached the stairs leading to the second floor. Located there were the reference room and literature section. These stairs were also wide. There were nine walking steps. The tread was wide and the incline gradual. On the wall side of these stairs was another ramp. At the top of the ramp was imbedded another plaque, which read:

THIS RAMP DONATED TO THE HANDICAPPED
BY THE KNIGHTS OF COLUMBUS 1971

"Was there much silver, Catherine?"

"Never have I seen so much silver. But it seems I wasn't the only girl at St. Hilda's who was out of line last week. There were four of us. Miss Vertue was there talking to the cook. She was wearing a pink pants-suit."

"Miss Vertue in a pink pants-suit? I can't imagine her in anything but navy-blue and white," mused Laura.

✳ ✳ ✳ ✳ ✳

This was Catherine's day for looking at statues. She was now scrutinizing the one standing on the corner of the second-floor landing. It was in an alcove that separated the arch leading to the reading-room from the stairwell.

"Laura, how many Saturday afternoons have we been coming here?"

"You mean to the second floor? Well, we abandoned the children's section in the sixth grade."

"So we've been passing this statue on the second-floor landing for almost two years?"

"That's right."

Catherine stepped back as she studied the statue. The statue itself stood on a pedestal almost two feet high. The figure was of a male without clothes except for a touch which had been added later— plastic ivy leaves draped artfully around its midriff. The effect was interesting.

"Did you ever wonder why that statue was wearing those ivy leaves?"

"Sure," said Laura, "every time we pass it."

"Well, I'm going to find out! You stand guard, and if you see or hear anyone coming, whistle something."

Both girls laughed as Catherine climbed onto the pedestal base. "Laura, these plastic leaves are full of dust. They're fixed on here with florist's wire. I'll have to untwist them."

"Hurry up, Catherine."

"There, I've got them. Laura, you'll never guess what's underneath. More leaves, only these ones are grape leaves and they are carved out of marble!"

"I hear someone coming, Catherine. Hurry." And as Laura whistled loudly, Catherine wrapped the cluster of plastic leaves around the head of the curly-haired statue. She gave the leaves a quick adjustment, tilted them at a rakish angle, jumped down, and assumed a sedate position behind Laura's wheel-chair. The man coming from the reference room gave them a kindly smile. He did not notice the statue.

The girls were still laughing as they entered the reading-room.

"I'll meet you in the literature section in a while," Catherine announced; "I'm going to the science reference room."

22

"Catherine, we don't have homework for science class."

"I know. I have some make-up work to do. Besides, maybe I'll check on male anatomy!" They chuckled.

But anatomy, most particularly the study of the male form, was not what was concerning Catherine. It was a piece of paper she had in her jacket pocket on which there was written a long word: "pseudo-hypertrophic." Underneath the word her mother had written Laura's name. Catherine had found the paper in her mother's desk when she was looking for some stamps. She knew it had something to do with Laura's condition, a condition which Catherine knew by one name only, muscular dystrophy. She wanted to know what that other word meant.

A man behind the desk asked her if he could help.

"Yes, I'd like to see a medical dictionary."

The man gestured toward the correct shelf.

"Thank you," said Catherine. After a brief perusal she pulled a book. Its title: *The American Medical Dictionary, 20th Edition.* Her finger traced the edge of the tabulated pages until she got to P. She opened the book and leafed quickly through until her eyes found that word. She read:

> pseudohypertrophy (su-do-hi-per'tro-fe) False hypertrophy; increase of size without true hypertrophy. *muscular p.,* pseudo-hypertrophic paralysis. See 'paralysis'.

Catherine had played the dictionary game before, the one where you looked up one word and that led to looking up another word, and another, and another. Methodically she flipped the pages to 'paralysis'. There were more than three columns listed under that one word. Her eyes followed the columns down until she came to 'pseudo-hypertrophic muscular p.' She read on:

> A chronic disease characterized by enlargement without true hypertrophy of the muscles, with paralysis due to disturbance of nutrition, producing atrophy of the muscle fibres with hypertro-phy of the connective tissue and fatty infiltration. The disease occurs usually late in childhood, and is marked by various de-formities, lordosis, and a peculiar swaying gait with the legs kept far apart. The paralysis progressively increases, ending in death, which is usually due to respiratory weakness.

Catherine read the last sentence again. Then she read it again. She slammed the book shut. She said aloud, "That can't be true. That can't have anything to do with Laura."

The room was empty except for the man at the desk. He didn't seem to hear her.

Catherine stared at the volume lying before her. It was burgundy-colored and worn. She picked it up again and turned to the front. She read: 'Reprinted June, 1945, and February, 1946.' "Besides," she declared to an almost empty room, "that book is old. They did not even have the Salk vaccine for polio then." She rose abruptly and marched out of the room, knowing that what she had just read could not pertain to Laura.

Catherine found Laura parked in the section marked 'Biographies.

"Hi Cath, I just found a book about Sarah Bernhardt. She was a famous actress. Did you know she actually slept in a coffin?"

"I don't know why you would find *that* so interesting," Catherine snapped. "Let's get out of here."

"But you haven't found any books to take out. We just got here."

"I just don't feel like being in this dusty old place this afternoon. Come on, let's check out your books and go."

Laura agreed. She was used to her sister, and one of the things she knew was that Catherine was unpredictable. She also knew that Catherine never stayed irritable for long. By the time they got to the sidewalk in front of the library, Catherine's gentle nature had returned.

Catherine pointed the wheel-chair in the direction of the bakery. That was where they always went after they left the library. Desserts were rarely served in the Devon household, so it was a weekly treat both girls looked forward to.

They were an interesting pair. Catherine strode purposefully, manipulating with ease and authority her sister's wheel-chair. Both were pretty, but Catherine knew Laura to be the prettier of the two. Her hair was long and thick and, unlike Catherine's which was unmanageably curly, fell in soft waves. Her features were not defined with the sharpness of her twin's. Laura's face was young for her years, where Catherine looked old beyond hers. Catherine's mother said she would be a handsome woman. She did not resent the fact her sister was prettier, for she did not think much about her own appearance, but enjoyed the compliments Laura drew on hers.

They were used to being stared at. They had long ago learned that people responded in strange ways to wheel-chairs. In fact they had made a study of them and divided them into groups. It was true that many people were occupied with their own concerns and too busy to make any particular note of Laura and her sister at all. But then there were those who became embarrassed upon seeing a girl being pushed in a wheel-chair, quickly averting their eyes, and sometimes even crossing the street to avoid confrontation. And then there were the people who did not notice Catherine at all, but were solicitous of Laura, offering her sympathy and sometimes other things. This was the group both Laura and Catherine found difficult. The group they welcomed were those who smiled and said, hello.

As they stood at the corner waiting for the light to change, the sweet fragrance of baked goods hot from the oven invited them to hurry. "The Cosmopolitan System of Bakeries," it was called. It stood on the corner of a busy intersection and was always crowded. Saturdays were worst. Its offerings were wide and varied: in breads, everything from Russian pumpernickel to Vienna rolls; in pastries, from French puffs to jelly doughnuts. Laura and Catherine made their way into the store, took a number, and as they waited were intent on making a choice. A very tall woman with a heavy torso and skinny legs approached. Her dress was white, with wide stripes of yellow, green, and blue running diagonally across her front, from the left shoulder to the hem. She looked like a flapping flag as she descended on the girls.

"I think that woman is going to be a problem, Laura," whispered Catherine hurriedly.

"I think so too. It's O.K., I can manage," Laura whispered back.

The woman put her face, heavy with make-up, close to Laura's. "You poor thing," she said as her hand rested on Laura's shoulder.

"It all started when my sister and I were abandoned."

"No!" exclaimed the woman, waiting to hear more.

"Yes, you see my mother married a sailor who left her because the sea was calling to him. My mother could not face the responsibility of raising two infants all by herself, so she left us in a basket on the steps of the orphanage."

The woman was beginning to look uncomfortable. Laura continued, "We've been there ever since. Mother wrote us once. She told us she was sorry, she had run off to Portugal with a gypsy king and was very happy."

The woman had begun to back away.

"It's all right at the orphanage, though. We're quite happy there. On our birthday we get to have jam on our toast."

The woman now had almost backed her way to the door. She turned and left hurriedly.

The baker called Laura's and Catherine's number.

"I don't think she'll do that any more, Laura. I think we should have a chocolate eclair."

"I think that *that* is a very good choice!"

✳ ✳ ✳ ✳ ✳

The day could not have been more perfect for an outing in the park. The sun was shining and the sky was blue and cloudless. Crocuses popped through the lawn, splashes of purple, white, and yellow, like colored buttons tossed on a plush carpet. Catherine and Laura munched on eclairs to the accompaniment of the whomp of tennis balls lobbed across the courts. Catherine propped her feet against the handle of the down-end of a teeter-totter, stretched out on the plank, and felt the sun of her face. Polishing off the last bite of her eclair she announced, "I think I'll try a jelly doughnut next time. These are pretty hard to eat—look where I've slopped on my jacket. Lucky Miss Vertue can't see me now."

Laura was not listening. She was watching a large black poodle joyfully flush the first crop of spring robins from beds of shrubs surrounding the park. "I think when I come back, I'll come back as a poodle."

"What are you talking about?"

"Reincarnation, Catherine. I'm talking about reincarnation."

"Oh, not you, too! You mean that when you die, you think your soul comes back in another body or in another form? Ms. Freeman is always talking about that. The last time I played badly, she said she was coming back as an airport mechanic who wears ear-muffs to keep out sounds. She thinks her cat was a person last time around . . . . If there is such a thing, I would like to come back as a candy-maker!"

"Seriously, Catherine, what would you come back as?"

"I'd come back as somebody famous. I'd like to be famous. I know, I'd like to be a famous actress that's loved and adored by the world."

"You mean like Sarah Bernhardt. Everyone adored her. At least they did when she was on the stage."

"Don't tell me we're back on the subject of *her* again. She may have been a great actress but anyone that would want to sleep in a coffin would have to be very strange. I don't think I would have liked her."

"When she was a little girl she almost died. Ever after that she was convinced she wasn't going to live long . . . , even though it turned out she did. Anyway, I think I can understand why she slept in a coffin. Maybe she was just practising. I mean maybe she was getting used to the idea of dying."

"Talking about her gives me the spooks. Let's change the subject. What do you want to be when you grow up?"

"I'd like to be a writer. Maybe a historian. I like to learn about things that happened. And I'd rather *write* about famous people than *be* a famous person. So many famous people seem to be unlucky. I was asking Dad about St. Hilda last night, and he showed me a book written by a man named Bede. He lived almost thirteen hundred years ago. He wrote about England, its saints and kings, from 449 A.D. to his own time. If he hadn't done that, lots of information about what people did then would have been lost. Just think, Catherine, after all

those years people are still reading his book, and not just because it's there, but because it's good!"

"What did you find out about old St. Hilda?" Catherine asked, with no great enthusiasm.

"She was older than Bede by about sixty years. After she served as an Abbess in northern England she founded a monastery of her own. She was so wise, even kings would ask her for advice. And she was loved by poor people, too."

"But what was her miracle? In order to be a saint, doesn't there have to be some miracle?" asked Catherine.

"Well, Bede, who wrote about her, reported that God sent her a long sickness to make her stronger in her weakness."

"I don't understand that, Laura."

"I think it's sort of like a test."

"A test for what?"

"A test to see if even in her illness she would continue to love God and serve Him."

"Well, did she?"

"Yes, every day for more than six years. Then she died."

"But you still haven't told me the miracle, Laura."

"The miracle was that the night of her death she appeared in a vision to a nun who lived several miles away. This nun saw St. Hilda's soul in a heavenly light being borne up to heaven. And in the same convent where St. Hilda died, another nun saw a similar vision and woke up the other nuns to pray for her. These nuns were in a different part of the convent and did not hear of her death until morning."

"So you mean they knew she died before they had been told?"

"Yes. That's the way Bede told it in the history he wrote."

"Laura, I think you must be the only student at St. Hilda's who actually ever read of St. Hilda."

"Oh, I'm sure that before, when they used to teach religion there, *all* the girls studied about St. Hilda," laughed Laura.

"Yes, but not willingly," Catherine laughed back, "I really don't understand you sometimes, Laura. You're always looking back. Not me, I'll be happy when I never have to see that school again . . . . I'm looking ahead!"

"Let's go home, Catherine. I'm getting tired, and *you* have to practise."

V

Catherine had a funny nervous feeling in the pit of her stomach as she approached the conservatory. She always had that feeling before her music lesson. For Catherine was a little afraid of Ms. Freeman. Catherine had a good deal of respect for her and wanted very much, perhaps too much, to earn her approval.

The medley of sounds coming from the practice-rooms and studios reassured her somehow. Perhaps it was because Catherine was reminded that behind the violins, flutes, clarinets, voices, and pianos, there was an aspiring student. Or maybe it was because the sounds created a comforting kind of music of their own. She bit her lip nervously as she knocked lightly on the studio door. She heard Ms. Freeman's voice respond to the knock.

"Come in, Catherine."

And Catherine always felt better once she entered the room. It was a grand room! Today the afternoon sun was flooding it with warmth. The four walls were covered with black-framed photographs. Some of the people in the photographs Catherine recognized. She had seen their faces on record jackets she had at home. Some of the photographs were signed with special greetings to her teacher. On the window wall hung a huge oil portrait of Ms. Freeman. She was wearing a gown of ice-blue, one that exactly matched the hue of her eyes. Catherine did not know when the picture had been painted, but guessed it must have been some time ago, for it was a younger Ms. Freeman in the painting. Even now she was beautiful. She was tall and very slim. Her skin was creamy-white, her cheeks lightly rouged; but for that, she wore no makeup. Her deep-set eyes were her outstanding feature. They could look at you and laugh, or they could look at you and make you shiver.

The piano rested on an oriental rug and stood in the middle of the room. It was a concert grand, and over its ebony lid was thrown a piano-scarf, of a rich rose color and so large it hung, with fringed edges, several inches below the lid. Covering much of the surface were exquisitely embroidered poppies in soft pastel shades of pink, green, and blue. Ms. Freeman had been to China, and it was there she found the piano-scarf. The only time it was taken off the piano was when Catherine had succeeded in playing one of her pieces very, very well. Then Ms. Freeman would fold it ceremoniously as she announced to

Catherine, "Now the piece is ready to be listened to with the lid *up!*"

When that happened, Catherine knew she had had a good lesson.

"Hello Catherine! Isn't it a magnificent day! Don't you just love this time of the year? It reminds me of . . . ," and she broke off seeing that Catherine understood. "Do sit down! Well, what pleasant musical surprise does my little friend have for me today? Let us start with your old favorite, Catherine. Play C-Major scale, four octaves, please, and end with its cadence."

Laura's idea of rewarding Catherine with M & M's had worked. For on that day Catherine had discovered some pleasure in playing scales. She had practised them every day since, and played them now with ease. As Ms. Freeman continued to drill Catherine, her confidence and spirit grew.

Ms. Freeman put her fingers to her lips and kissed them twice. "I love you, Catherine, I love you," she exclaimed as she blew her two kisses. "At last! You have conquered your scales—*all* your scales, including C-Major. Congratulations!"

Catherine said a silent prayer of thanks to Laura.

"I'd like to work on the Schumann," Ms. Freeman announced. "We'll begin with number 28, please."

One of the pieces Catherine was learning was from a collection called an "Album for the Young." This piece was simply called, "In Memoriam." It was marked by three stars, and at the bottom of the page was written the comment, "The day of Mendelssohn's death."

Ms. Freeman allowed Catherine to play the piece through without interruption. "Catherine, this appears on the surface to be a very simple piece, but though the piece appears simple, I do not want you to believe it was written by a very simple man. No, Schumann had written many grander works before he wrote this. But in this little piece is beautiful poetry . . . , poetry of the soul, Catherine. He wrote it to the memory of one of his dearest friends, Felix Mendelssohn, some of whose pieces you remember studying. Mendelssohn died very suddenly and at a rather young age. Schumann was so despondent over his friend's death he was unable to compose music again for several months. It is not an accident this song sounds as though Mendelssohn himself wrote it. Imitating Mendelssohn's style was Schumann's way of paying tribute to his friend's memory. So you see, Catherine, this was not just a casual little piece Schumann wrote in a hurry. He was giving expression to some very deep feelings. Play the piece again, Catherine, and see if you can capture the feeling as you play."

Catherine was not sure she understood. She was interrupted after playing one line.

"No, no, no! That is not it at all. Feel the music in your head, Catherine, and it will come through in the melody. Remember, some of our

deepest feelings are ones we hold in. Schumann was far too complicated a man to be obvious. You were being just that. Obvious. Like a gospel song. Gospel songs are fine in their place, but this is not what we want to hear in this music!"

She wondered what Ms. Freeman would know of gospel music. Catherine knew something of it because, when preparing supper, she and her mother often sang the familiar tunes along with the local gospel radio station. And singing those tunes with her mother was fun. Thinking of that, she began again.

Ms. Freeman was laughing. "Catherine, I'm afraid you are not capturing the feeling. But your interpretation reminds me of performances I once gave."

Catherine now was puzzled. She could not imagine what Ms. Freeman was talking about.

"I cut my music teeth on gospel music. I'd be willing to wager you never would have guessed that. You see, my father was a minister. I learned to play chords on the church piano before I learned to read words. I played hymns for the congregation all my growing-up years. Stand up for a minute and I'll demonstrate."

And with that, that elegant lady—the lady Catherine thought the most dignified she'd ever known—did something which took Catherine completely by surprise. She played the most rousing, foot-stomping chorus of "Abide With Me" that she had ever heard.

"Do you know it, Catherine? Sing and I'll play it again!" And there, in the middle of the sunshiny afternoon, with the window open to the violinists, the flutists, the clarinetists, the vocalists, and the pianists, teacher and student sang three rousing verses of "Abide With Me." The other students and their instructors must have listened in some confusion.

"Catherine, I don't know if it is this beautiful spring afternoon, or the fact that you played your scales so well that has brought such fun to this lesson. I do know that I have enjoyed it immensely. I also know we had better leave the Schumann for now. Give it some thought and we'll work on it at your next lesson. Now let us direct our attention to some Bach."

Catherine was working on a two-part Invention. She enjoyed playing it, for it was like math and made sense to her. She felt relief at playing something she could understand. She could hear the two voices singing with and around each other. Laura's singing the melody lines as she practised had helped her define and separate them. The voices sang out clean and true. When Ms. Freeman complimented her on the voice work, she again felt grateful to Laura.

The rest of the lesson progressed as usual.

"Catherine, continue working like this and you might get another 'first' on your piano exam!"

"I would like to, but, Ms. Freeman . . . ."

"Yes, do you have some doubts?"

"I'm nervous about the Schumann. I really don't understand what is wanted."

"Don't play the piece for what *I* want. Play it for what you *feel*."

"But you said to hold my feelings in. How? When I'm happy, I laugh. When I'm sad, I cry. When I'm angry, I yell. Those feelings show. How can I express feelings if I don't show them?"

"Ah, but Catherine, how do you show deep affection for a friend? Or how do you show love for a parent? How do you show sadness at the loss of a friend? These are things you feel. And in this case you show what you are feeling through the music. I can understand your confusion. Many of these things we learn simply by getting older. That's why the Schumann is not simple. It requires understanding. Don't worry, Catherine, just let it brew in your head and I'm certain you will sort it out. What you need now is a little time."

"Are you sure, Ms. Freeman?"

"Yes, Catherine, I'm sure. Keep up the good work and I will see you next week."

Catherine felt good about her lesson. Since it had gone so well, she could not understand why she was not feeling better. Then she realized her throat was scratchy and sore, and her face felt hot. It was then she noticed she was still wearing Laura's sweater. Catherine had almost made them late again that morning, and, as they were rushing to the room, she realized she had forgotten her cardigan. Laura insisted she wear hers, saying Miss Vertue would not notice if she did not have hers, but she'd certainly notice if Catherine appeared without one. Catherine, not relishing the idea of polishing more silver, agreed. Laura had been right. Miss Vertue did not notice.

Catherine shivered. The late afternoon had suddenly turned cold. It felt more like winter again, and Catherine hoped Laura had not needed the sweater. Her anxiety and the chill made her walk faster.

VI

Laura and Catherine were dressed alike. That was unusual, for they rarely were, each having different and distinctive tastes. This time it was not a matter of choice. Laura sat in her wheel-chair wearing a white hospital gown that was open at the back and tied at the nape of her neck. Catherine dangled her legs over the edge of an examining table wearing a matching gown. As they waited for a doctor to come in, their father waited in the reception room of the emergency entrance of City General Hospital.

Very atypically, Laura was very crabby: "Isn't this an ugly little room, Catherine? No windows and that awful fluorescent light. Look, it makes my arms look purple. Even if you were well, you couldn't look good under that light. And why are hospitals so crazy about that hideous green paint? It's the same green they use in the halls at St. Hilda's. I'm glad I don't have stomach flu. That color would really make me throw up. Catherine, see if this thing is closed in the back. I feel stupid in this dumb gown."

"Sure," said Catherine, jumping down off the table. She padded over to the wheel-chair and checked her sister's back. "Yes, it's closed. I feel stupid too. I wonder what genius designed these?"

"I wonder if that doctor is going to keep me in the hospital," Laura mused, knowing it was a possibility. Simple colds were not simple for her. She had been hospitalized in the past for similar complaints. Laura was all too familiar with "hospital green." She was also familiar with hospital routine. "Catherine, get off that scale and get back onto the table. A nurse will be coming in any minute to take your temperature."

Catherine hopped back onto the table. "It's boring in here. There's nothing to do. I know . . . . I spy, with my little eye, something that begins with 'L.' "

She launched into a game they used to play when they were little. The object of the game was for the contestant to guess what the player was looking at—an object which began with that letter.

"I don't feel like playing 'I Spy.' I feel terrible."

"So do I, but it would help the time pass."

"All right, Cath. I guess, 'light.' "

"No, that's not it."

"Linoleum?"

"Nope."

"Lotion?"

"Uh, unh."

"I give up!"

"Laura, you can't give up now. You just got started."

A nurse came into the room. She was round and jolly. "Here, girls, stick these thermometers in your mouths. They will keep you quiet for a moment. I *could* tell you, you are disturbing the patients around here who can't sleep . . . , but I won't. You might be doing us a service by keeping some resident physicians awake!"

"Do I hear someone insulting the profession?" asked a young doctor as he entered the room. "Hello girls. How are we tonight?"

"If 'we' were fine, 'we' would not be here," retorted Catherine.

The doctor looked amused. "I think I learned one thing tonight— not to ask dumb questions."

The girls laughed and felt more relaxed.

The doctor examined them. He tapped their chests, looked into their ears and throats, read their temperatures, and announced, "I believe you both have the same virus. I want throat cultures taken. You have twin fevers but you won't get twin treatment. You, young lady," he said, looking at Laura, "will be a guest in the hospital tonight. We want to keep you under observation." He looked at Catherine: "I'll prescribe some medication for you. You should be feeling better soon. And now I'm going to talk to your Dad. Excuse me, the nurse will tell you what to do."

"Laura, if I had given you your sweater back, maybe you wouldn't have gotten sick. I feel awful about that and now you have to stay. I'm sorry."

"I don't want you to feel responsible, Cath. Your having my sweater had nothing to do with me getting this bug. Remember, you got sick too, and you *had* the sweater. I wasn't even outside today. Mom picked me up right after school. And a lot of other girls at school are sick, too."

"I still wish you could come home."

"So do I, but I'm used to this routine, Catherine."

The nurse interrupted the girls. "You may get dressed," she said looking at Catherine. "Your father can meet you in the lounge after he sees his other daughter. Laura, I'll take you with me."

Catherine hugged Laura. "I love you, Laura. Come home soon."

"I love you too, Catherine," and, as the nurse wheeled her out of the room, Laura called, "Oh Catherine, what was it?"

"What was what?"

"The 'L' in 'I Spy.' "

"Laura, the word was 'Laura.' "

"Well, tell me."

"I just did."

"Oh Catherine, you mean it was *me*. That's not fair. I can't see me!"

"I know, but *I* can!"

They were both grinning as the nurse wheeled Laura down the hall.

✳ ✳ ✳ ✳ ✳

Catherine could tell that her father was worried. She could tell by the way he absently pulled on his chin as he waited for the light to change. And the thinking line that appeared vertically along his brow only when he was concerned, was there now. Ordinarily when they drove in the van, her father pushed buttons on the car radio looking for news reports. Tonight they drove home without the radio. Catherine knew, too, it was her parents' concern for Laura that had brought them to the hospital. Catherine could have gone to the family doctor. Meanwhile, her mother brooded at home while taking care of Jeff.

The van pulled up the driveway to the front of the house. It felt strange not having Laura there. "Laura will be fine, won't she, Dad?"

"The doctor said it would be better to have her there, where they can keep an eye on her. Now, how are you doing? You look flushed. I'll take care of you, young lady!" With that, he scooped her out of the van-seat and carried her up the walk.

"I can walk, Dad!"

"Don't deny your father the privilege of showing his gorgeous daughter how strong he is!"

When he placed her on the living-room couch, she was glad he had carried her. She felt dizzy and weak. Jeff and her mother appeared from the kitchen.

"Catherine, I want to get you into bed. Peter, I want to go to the hospital. I've fixed a light supper for you and Jeff. Mrs. Cameron will stay with Jeff and Catherine until we get home."

So her father *had* phoned from the hospital. He was thoughtful that way, thought Catherine.

"How long is Laura going to be in the hospital?" asked Jeff. He was already in his pajamas, having had his bath and a shampoo. His hair was still wet. Catherine thought he looked like a cocker spaniel. She found herself feeling warm thoughts toward him.

Her father replied, "Just until she gets over her virus, Jeff. They can take better care of her there. Come on, let's go get that supper. Your Mom wants to get to the hospital." He read Jeff's mind. "And no, you can't go and see her; she's in the isolation ward, and only your mother and I are allowed to visit. And even if she weren't, they don't allow visitors under sixteen. Sorry, Jeff, I know you'd like to see her. Come, let's go eat."

Catherine lay in bed and looked at the ceiling. She could hear Jeff and Mrs. Cameron talking in the living-room. Mrs. Cameron was more than nice. She was an elderly lady, with white hair and a kind face, and though she'd been on this side of the Atlantic for forty years, she spoke with a fresh, thick Scots brogue. Catherine loved to listen to her. She had been a neighbor many years and was like another grandmother to the Devon children. When she sat with them she always came with treats. Sometimes she brought delicious sweet oatmeal cookies. Sometimes she brought buttery Scotch shortbread. She always brought a smile. The girls and Jeffrey had long had a special name for her: 'Mrs. Happy.'

Jeff appeared at the bedroom door. "Look what Mrs. Happy brought me!" He was holding a flat, red-plaid box: MACKINTOSH toffee."

That was nice of her, Jeff."

"I'll share it with you."

"That's nice of you, Jeff, but I really don't care for any. My jaw feels too weak to chew."

"Boy, you really must be sick!" Jeff had taken the toffee from out of its box and was unwrapping the wax-paper. The candy itself was rectangular and marked off in squares. But the markings on the toffee were decorative, not functional. It was impossible to break the hunk apart on the lines. Jeff walked over to the window sill and began hammering the toffee against it.

"Jeff, don't break it that way!"

"What other way is there?"

"Wrap it up again."

"Why? I want to eat it now!"

"I know, but it's easier to break the toffee when it's in the box . . . . There. Now hit the box against the end of my bed. It won't hurt the metal bedstead. One hard crack and you'll have lots of little pieces."

Jeff followed Catherine's instructions. "Gee, you were right! And this way you don't lose any crumbs. You can lick them off the paper. Why didn't I think of that? Thanks, Cath."

"It took me a long time to figure out that system. I used to take the toffee out of the wrapper and smash it on the sidewalk. Then I'd have to pick little bits of toffee out of the cracks. And I usually got a lot of little rocks sticking in the big pieces. So I wasn't always so smart!"

Jeff laughed and looked grateful. He munched as he swung in the hanging-basket chair. "Will Laura be O.K.?"

"Of course she will. You know how she is with colds . . . . Jeff, stop swinging in that chair. It's making me dizzy."

"Well then, close your eyes."

Catherine did.

"I miss Laura, Catherine."

"I know," she said, and then she fell asleep.

VII

It was Saturday, and almost a week had gone by since the girls had become ill. Catherine recovered quickly enough to finish out the school week, but Laura was still in the hospital. Laura was not doing well. She had pneumonia. And things were not going well in the Devon household. Catherine's father didn't talk to her at all, and her mother was irritable.

Catherine sat across the table looking at Jeff. He was the only person in the house worth talking to now, Catherine thought, as she slurped the remaining dregs of her milkshake through her straw.

"Catherine, please stop that. It is getting on my nerves," her mother snapped.

She did, and as she exchanged a quiet look of resignation with her brother her glance said, *everything* seemed to get on her mother's nerves these days.

"Catherine, do you have homework?"

"Nothing pressing, Mother." That was not exactly true, but she did not feel like doing homework right then. She did not feel like doing anything. She missed Laura.

"You have not practised all week. After lunch, would you please do so?"

"Yes, Mother," Catherine sighed.

"Don't act so put upon. In three days you have a lesson and in a little more than a month, a piano exam."

"Mom, you don't need to tell me that. I'm well aware of those facts."

Her father interjected, "Enough, Catherine, I won't have you using that tone."

Catherine fell silent. Her mother took note of this.

"I'm sorry, Kate. I've been a bit short these days. Things will be better when . . . ." Her voice trailed off. Mrs. Devon pulled herself up short and announced with false brightness, "After your practice, I have a surprise for you!"

"For me?" Catherine was surprised. It did not feel like the sort of day for surprises.

"Yes, for you. Now run and practise." She looked at her husband. "You can take Jeff to the park for his game. I'll clear the table. Everybody, scoot!"

Catherine approached the piano with reluctance. The threat of an imminent lesson was not enough incentive to make her want to practise. For the truth was that Catherine no longer cared. The only thing she cared about was having Laura home again. Her fingers tried C-Major scale. They ran an octave and stumbled. She tried and failed again.

"It's obvious I can't play scales today," she thought to herself, "and I know I can't play the Schumann. I'll try the Bach." She began to play. She tried to imagine she could hear Laura singing the voices. It didn't work. She left the piano abruptly and threw herself on the couch. She heard her mother's brisk step in the hall.

"I can't practise *for* you," her mother sighed, "and I can see you are not going to accomplish anything in your present state. Come to your bedroom and I'll show you my surprise. Perhaps you'll be able to practise better after supper."

They walked down the hall to the girls' bedroom. Laura's bed was littered with wallpaper books, sample paint colors, swatches of curtain fabrics, and carpet samples.

"What is all this, Mother?"

"Your Dad and I thought this would be the perfect time to redecorate your room. If we do it now, Laura won't have to breathe paint fumes or accommodate herself to the mess. And it's spring break at the college, so your Dad will be able to help us."

"But Mom, the room is nice just the way it is!"

"The room has not been painted since you were little girls. It has to be done. Come, Kate, help me pick a color. Let's decide on a color first. Then we'd better pick the rug, then the wallpaper and the curtains."

"No, I don't want to pick a color. The room is nice the way it is now. I don't want to change it!"

"Catherine, Laura will love it. It will be such a nice surprise for her. Both of you are fond of yellow. This is such a sunny room. Yellow would be good in here."

"Mom, the room is cosy and comfortable. I don't want it all new and cosmetic. Please, let's leave the room alone."

"I think you should have new bedspreads."

"Mom, you aren't listening to me. I don't want to change this room."

"Catherine, you are not being reasonable!"

"What's so reasonable about redecorating a room when one of your daughters is in the hospital?"

Suddenly her mother's eyes filled with tears. She sat down on Catherine's bed: "Catherine, this will help all of us occupy ourselves while we wait for Laura to come home. I need to fill the moments between hospital visits."

"Well I don't!"

"Catherine, if you won't help me pick what you want, your father and I will go ahead and choose for you," her mother said softly.

"I'm sorry, Mom. Do what you want. I've told you how I feel."

"I'm sorry too, Catherine, but I'm not going to change my mind."

"May I go now, Mom?"

"Yes, Kate, you may."

Catherine did not feel angry; she felt terrible and empty. She sat on the front-porch step and waited for something to happen. Something finally did. Jeff and her Dad came home. She grunted as Jeff stepped over her legs and disappeared inside the house. In a few minutes he returned carrying something.

"What have you got, Jeff?" She saw what he was carrying as soon as he turned around. It was the ant-farm he had been given for his birthday a year ago. White sand was sandwiched between two layers of glass contained in a case, the top of which was empty. The case had a lid that covered small holes through which bits of food and sugar water could be dropped. Jeff had set the ant-farm on the window sill over the kitchen sink. The Devons had for several months watched the insects busily construct tunnels and rooms. The ants slowly died out and were carted off to the ant cemetery until there was no ant left to carry off the last one. The ant-farm had remained on the window sill ever since.

"Where are you going with that?" Catherine asked, more out of boredom than anything else.

"I'm going to catch myself an ant."

"And then what are you going to do?" she asked again, now curious.

"I'm going to catch myself another one."

"Jeff, you can't just put any old ants together. They have to come from the same colony. If they don't, they'll kill each other."

"I know," Jeff replied matter-of-factly.

"Well how are you going to tell if the ants are from the same colony?"

"Easy," said Jeff.

"How?"

"I'll just find an ant and follow him home!"

Catherine had to admit that was a very good idea. She was surprised her brother could be so resourceful.

"Can I help?" she asked.

"Sure. I think I saw some ants crawling around here in the crack of this bottom step."

"You did. I was watching them before you came home from the game. Let's track one to its home."

Jeff and Catherine watched ants for a long time. Mostly the ants scurried around the cement track. There did not seem to be a pattern to the insects' movements. One did venture out on a safari through the grass but they lost it in the jungle. Another one set a zig-zag course down the front walk but became confused when it reached the curb. They watched it go up and down the curb several times and finally decided that that ant had no sense of direction, and would never lead them to the colony.

"Jeff, you had a good idea but those ants aren't cooperating. I'm getting tired of watching ants."

"Me too."

"What should we do now?"

"Have you ever been to that pet store across from the grocery?"

"Not for a long time."

"The store has new owners," Jeff said, "and they've got a tame raccoon. The people let you hold him. It's fun . . . he's really cute! Do you want to go and see him?"

"Yes, I would. Raccoons have sharp teeth. Doesn't he bite?"

"No, never. His paws look like hands. He puts his paw on your face but he never scratches. They call him O'Henry because they give him a candy bar every day!"

"Lucky raccoon!"

"I'll say. And wait 'til you see him. Boy, is he fat!"

"I bet! Is he heavy?" She was enjoying this kid-talk.

"Quite, but he holds himself up pretty well."

They headed in the direction of the pet shop.

"Catherine, do you like oatmeal?"

"It's O.K. I like cream-of-wheat better. Why?"

"There's this box-top offer that comes with oatmeal. If you send in two box-tops and a quarter, they'll send you a package of sea-monkey eggs. I have one box-top saved, but it's taking a long time to get the second one. Mom got a big box."

"I'll eat oatmeal for you, and Mom will let me make cookies. They take quite a lot of oatmeal. What are sea-monkeys?"

"The back of the box says they come in a package. You drop the eggs in a jar of water, and in a little while they hatch."

"Do they look like monkeys?"

"I don't know. The box didn't have a picture."

"Hmm, I'd like to see them too. I'll eat a lot of oatmeal!"

"Thanks, Cath. I wonder how long it will take to finish it?"

The raccoon delighted Catherine. The owners, a man and his wife, let her hold him, and Catherine giggled as the pet crawled up on her shoulder and wrapped his paws around her neck. "Oh Jeff, we'll have to bring Laura!"

"I hope soon," Jeff answered.

Catherine's mood changed suddenly. "We have to go home. Mom said she'd serve supper early. They want to get to the hospital."

On the way home Jeff skipped the cracks in the sidewalk, chanting as he jumped:

"If you step on a crack,
You break your mother's back.
If you step on a line,
You break your mother's spine."

"Why is Mom so crabby? She made me take my ant-farm off the window sill. It's been sitting there almost a year. Then all of a sudden, bang, she's giving me a lecture about clutter!"

"She gets this way when Laura's sick. Every time Laura is in the hospital she launches on a massive cleaning campaign. Now she's going to redecorate our bedroom, which is really dumb. The room is comfortable the way it is. It's strange enough . . . , not having Laura there. If she changes it, it won't feel like our room at all."

"Why don't you tell her that?"

"I did. I told her it was fine the way it was. She wouldn't listen, and said she and Dad would go ahead and decorate without my cooperation."

They walked along in silence. Catherine was thinking. It *had* been a pleasant afternoon, and for a little while at least, she had stopped worrying about her sister. And that day she had discovered her brother was better than nice: he was fun.

"Why didn't you go to the library this afternoon, Cath? You always go to the library Saturday afternoons."

"I didn't want to go alone," Catherine said.

"I'm sorry, Cath."

And Catherine knew he really was.

VIII

C atherine sat on the end of her bed which had been shoved into the middle of the room. She watched her father climb up the ladder and remove the peacock feathers. He took the hanging-basket chair from its hook and dropped it carefully on the floor. Then he pulled a pair of pliers from his rear pocket and quickly unscrewed the large hook. He opened a can of liquid plaster which was resting on the ladder's platform and, with a putty knife, filled in the large holes. Catherine had not yet accepted the fact that their room was to be changed, but had resigned herself to it. She had not anticipated, however, the removal of the hanging-basket chair.

"Why are you taking it down? Dad, that's the neatest thing in this room. Now you've ruined it completely!"

"Patience, Kate, we've got other plans for this hanging-basket chair!"

Catherine did not respond. She felt a hard, angry knot in her stomach. She could not understand how her parents could be so heartless. Angrily she turned away from her father. Why was it, she wondered, he found it so easy to take the chair down, when he had had so much difficulty putting it up? In fact, she observed, suddenly her dad had become an expert at wallpaper hanging and painting— handyman's jobs he had never been good at before. It was as though he enjoyed flaunting the room's transformation before her. And the room certainly was being transformed.

The wall against which the headboards of the beds rested had been hung with wallpaper, patterned with delicate yellow and white daisies. The window-wall opposite had the same treatment. Her father had painted the moldings a soft yellow. The bookshelf wall and the desk wall were painted; they picked up the same color. Her father had been stirring a bucket of white paint which, she assumed, he'd apply to the ceiling when he was through fixing the holes.

Now she directed her attention to her mother. Her mother had often joked that when she was through with the business of raising children, she could hire herself out as a painter. Catherine watched her dip her brush into a pail of yellow enamel and apply it to the narrow woodwork around the window pane. With one downward motion the paint brush drew a smooth line over the wood's surface. The paint did not spill off her brush onto the pane. Catherine watched her dip and paint, dip and paint, smooth, hypnotically. She worked her way from right to left and downward to the sill. Catherine interrupted the rhythm with a startled cry, "Mother, STOP!"

"Catherine, what is it?"

"Mom, you can't! You can't paint over Laura's name!"

"What on earth are you talking about?"

"Laura's name. Laura wrote her name on the bottom of the window sill when she was learning to print. Look here, Mom. See, it has a backwards 'L' and a backwards 'R.'"

And there it was, on the bottom of the sill: a child's printing spelling out the word, "JAUЯA."

"I know about that, Catherine. I've tried many times to wash it but Laura used a ball-point pen and it won't come off."

"Mother, how could you paint it out! If you do, you'll be covering over a memory."

"I'm sorry, Catherine, I'm going to continue painting and I will paint the window sill. I have memories in my head and heart. I don't need them on the sill."

"You are heartless!"

"I don't think you really believe that, Catherine," her father said, as evenly as he could.

"I'm trying to understand you, Catherine," her mother said, "but since the day you and Laura got sick, it has not been easy. I am beginning to wonder if you really *are* better. I was going to discuss this with you after supper, but since we seem to be having a discussion now, I may as well bring it up. I got another note from Miss Vertue today."

"Not another one," groaned Catherine.

"Yes, another one. She informed me you are not participating in class and that you have not turned in one assignment since you came back. Is this true?"

"Yes, it's true."

"That's not like you," her father said. "We are all missing Laura. But you know she is getting better care than we can give her here. Is that what's bothering you?"

"I'll tell you what's bothering me. Changing our room is bothering me!"

"Catherine, if you would involve yourself with homework and with the redecoration, you would find the time until your sister gets home passing more quickly."

"Your father is right. Time stops when you sit around moping. Today you are to get busy with that homework, and by the end of the week we expect you to be caught up at school. And now you might go and practise. You've not had a decent practice in a week."

"I'm not going to practise any more."

"What?"

"I mean I am quitting piano lessons."

Her father and mother looked at each other and, for a moment, said nothing. Then her mother said very quietly, "There is no point in our arguing with you about this. If you no longer wish to study music, you must phone Ms. Freeman and tell her so."

"You phone her, Mom."

"No, if that is your decision, you owe it to Ms. Freeman to phone her yourself."

"She won't like it."

"You'll have to work that out with her, Catherine," stated her dad, "and now I believe you have things to do other than sit here. Your mother and I can manage without your supervision."

Catherine stomped out of the room. So they did not require the pleasure of her company. That was fine with her; she wasn't particularly enjoying theirs. She was not happy over the prospect of phoning Ms. Freeman. In fact, she almost considered reversing her decision. But the thought of facing Ms. Freeman at a lesson with no practice was more terrifying than the thought of making the call. She looked up the phone number in the brown leather book which hung beside the telephone. She dialed slowly and hoped she would know what to say.

"Hello, Ms. Freeman?"

"Yes, is this Catherine?"

"Yes, Ms. Freeman. How are you?"

"I'm fine, Catherine. What may I do for you?"

Catherine stammered, "I will not—I mean, I don't want to—I'm not taking lessons any more, Ms. Freeman."

There was a long silence on the other end of the line. Catherine did not know what to say, so she said nothing.

"This comes as quite a surprise, Catherine."

"Yes, Ms. Freeman."

"You know I had high hopes for you on your piano exam."

"Yes, Ms. Freeman."

"Is something troubling you, Catherine?"

"No, nothing . . . . I just don't have time to practise."

"I see." There was another long pause. "You may feel differently about this another day. If you should change your mind, please let me know. I would be most happy to take you back."

"Thank you. Thank you very much. I will. Good-bye, Ms. Freeman."

"Good-bye, Catherine."

Catherine hung up the phone. That was not nearly as hard as she thought it would be. The hardest part was when she had been asked if something was bothering her. Catherine wondered if she should have told her teacher she could not practise without Laura. No, she decided abruptly: she would not have understood. Nobody would. She walked quickly down the hall and through the front door, and sat down on the front step. She hoped her mother or her father would not come out to nag her about homework, as she had no intention of doing any.

She did not know how long she had been sitting there. She did know what she had been thinking when she saw Miss Vertue come up the walk. It was that horrid word she had looked up in that old medical dictionary at the library: pseudohypertrophic. But then the last line of the definition replaced the word, the line which read, "The paralysis progressively increases, ending in death, which is usually due to respiratory weakness."

And now Laura had pneumonia. But she had had it before and been all right. Laura is going to be all right, she thought over and over. But will she be?

Miss Vertue walked purposefully up the walk. She was wearing the same pink pants-suit she had worn the day Catherine polished silver. Catherine felt as though she were dreaming. Miss Vertue did not look like herself in that outfit, and it seemed odd not to see her in the class-room or behind her desk. She had never visited the Devons before.

"Hello, Miss Vertue," Catherine said. The greeting sounded more like a question than a welcome.

"Hello, Catherine, do sit down. I'll just sit here on the step beside you. I suppose you are wondering why I'm here."

"Yes, Miss Vertue."

"I was hoping to catch you alone. Normally I would have paid your parents the courtesy of a phone call. I know they are very busy and concerned about Laura. I was afraid that if I phoned they might fuss, and I didn't want that, so I just took a chance . . . . I came to see *you*, Catherine."

Catherine steeled herself for a lecture.

Miss Vertue said in a rush, "If I were not so concerned about you I would not have felt compelled to have this talk, and if this visit hadn't been necessary, I suppose by the time you were my age, you would just remember me as the strict teacher you had in the eighth grade who had to search for her hankie when she got upset."

Catherine blushed.

"It's all right, Catherine. I did not come here to talk about me. I came here to talk about you. I have observed how your sister's illness has affected you, and it concerns me." There was a slight pause, and she continued: "You are afraid your sister is going to die, aren't you, Catherine?"

The word had been in Catherine's head and on her lips since Laura had been hospitalized. And now Miss Vertue had said it!

Catherine responded with a nod.

"I am right, am I not, Catherine?"

Catherine nodded once more.

"I thought so. It would be very strange indeed, if you didn't have that concern. It's a very real one. Laura *could* die. It might help to know that others share your concern . . . , all those who know and love her. And sometimes it helps to talk about our fears, and to know that others have them too . . . , to know we're not alone."

Catherine's throat felt tight. Miss Vertue's voice was soft as it continued: "We are all worried, Catherine. Not even the doctors know if Laura will live. But they have *hope* that she will. Your parents have it, and I'm certain if you could talk to Laura, she would tell you she has it too. You must do the same: have *hope*, Catherine! Now I want you to listen to me carefully, for what I have to say is important."

Catherine's eyes were moist. She said, in a voice that did not sound like her own, "Yes, Miss Vertue."

"I have taught many girls over the years, and of all of them I believe you to be one of the most gifted. I would not have told you that, Catherine, unless I felt you needed very much, right now, to hear it. But before I speak of one of those gifts, I would like to speak of Laura's gift . . . , Laura's gift to you. I think perhaps you are not aware of what it is, for if you were you would not be abusing it; which is what you are doing now."

Miss Vertue's reprimand did not feel like one. Her voice went soothingly on, "Laura, in her short life, has understood something about it that you are still working on. She understands that discipline helps give a meaning to life. As long as you are with Laura, I don't have to worry about you. Laura has enough discipline for the two of you: she sees to it you stay on course."

As Miss Vertue spoke, Catherine thought about Laura, the game with the M & M's, and now, quitting the piano.

Miss Vertue spotted her tears: "Here, my dear, use this." She opened her bag and handed her a fresh white handkerchief. "Since Laura has been in the hospital, what has happened saddens me. You are floating like a leaf on a pond. You are throwing Laura's gift away! If she knew that, Catherine, she would be hurt."

Catherine dabbed at quiet tears that wouldn't stop. Miss Vertue waited a moment and continued, "And before I leave, I would like to tell you of your gift to Laura."

"Mine?"

"Yes, yours, Catherine. You give to her your sense of fun, a necessary ingredient in everyone's life, but especially for her; for Laura's handicap makes it difficult to manufacture her own. Fun, Catherine!

A simple word, and each day you and your sister are together, you bring her laughter."

The two sat quietly together for several moments.

"Thank you, Miss Vertue," Catherine said quietly. "You know, I've been having trouble understanding and being understood by my folks."

"You are welcome, dear, and I am sure that's quite natural." Miss Vertue's voice assumed a slightly more businesslike tone: "I must leave . . . . Please don't get up."

She watched Miss Vertue go down the walk, get into her car, and drive away. Catherine had the thought of her encounter with Miss Vertue interrupted by the ring of the telephone. Absently she rose and walked slowly into the house. Her father stood in the kitchen with the phone to his ear. "I see," he said in a voice tight with strain. "Now? . . . . Yes, we'll be right there." He hung the receiver on the hook. "Catherine, that was the hospital. It's Laura . . . . They want your mother and me over there right away."

"Dad!"

"Your mother and I depend on you to manage while we are gone. Phone Mrs. Cameron. She'll stay with you and Jeff until we get home. We'll phone you from the hospital . . . . I'll get your mother. Catherine, we are depending upon you!"

She was phoning Mrs. Cameron when her mother and dad left. Catherine had never felt more alone.

IX

'Mrs. Happy' was in the den watching Lawrence Welk on the television. She had fixed Catherine and Jeff a delicious supper, but Catherine had hardly touched hers. She had watched Jeff eat every last morsel of his; he had helped her with the dishes, and now sat at the kitchen table taking cellophane off a large cardboard box on which a large grey blimp was pictured. The words over the picture said, 'Goodyear Blimp.' Under that was written: "Snap-together model kit. Lighted moving messages!" On the sides of the box the blimp's specifications were listed: "No gluing, no painting, pre-wired electrical harness, motor and flashing bulbs, requires batteries."

Catherine watched him lift the lid and examine the contents. There were many pieces of grey plastic, and a packet of black paper on which were written several messages in computer-print-out style. One said, "Winners Go Goodyear." Others said, "Season's Greetings!" "Happy Birthday to . . . ," and "Up, Up, and Away!" There were several pieces of paper left blank so the builder could make up his own messages.

Catherine watched Jeff pull the assembly instructions out of the box. He read the first line and began to assemble the model.

Catherine began pacing around the kitchen. "Jeff, I don't see how you can do that now! I mean, you really amaze me . . . . First you stuff yourself, and now you sit at this kitchen table building a blimp!"

"Why shouldn't I eat my supper? I was hungry."

"Laura is really sick, Jeff. How could you eat? Aren't you worried about her?"

"Yes. Yes, I am. What I am is scared."

"Then why, at a time like this, are you building a blimp?"

"Because," Jeff said reflectively, "because at a time like this, Cath, building a blimp is absolutely the safest thing to do."

Catherine looked at her brother. Jeff was right: at a time like this, building a blimp *was* absolutely the safest thing to do.

"Can I help?" she asked as she pulled a chair up to the table.

"Sure. I have to go get my pocket-knife and a file. Do you think we'll get it done tonight?"

"With the two of us working, I don't see why not!"

The two of them spent the better part of the evening bent over the kitchen table intent on their project. Mrs. Cameron came in to remind them about getting ready for bed. Catherine explained that they were almost finished and asked if they could stay up a little longer. 'Mrs. Happy' agreed.

"Look Jeff, all we have left to do are the messages."

The blimp had a panel on its side. The paper containing the message had to be inserted behind the opaque panel. When the blimp was snapped together and the battery turned on, the message was illuminated with light, and rotated slowly as it spun out the colored message.

"What's your message going to say, Jeff?"

"I'm not telling. I'll show it to you when I put it in the blimp."

"O.K., then I'll surprise you with mine!"

Catherine finished hers first.

"Can I put it in now?" she asked.

"Sure!"

Catherine's message spun out, "WELCOME HOME LAURA." Then Jeff inserted his, and it blinked, "GET WELL LAURA."

The two sat hypnotized for several moments as the message rotated around and around. Jeff asked suddenly, "Laura isn't going to die, is she, Catherine?"

Now he had said it . . . , that word, *die*.

Catherine did not answer.

"She isn't, is she, Cath?"

"I don't know, Jeff," Catherine said softly, "I still can't cope with it. We'd better get ready for bed."

Since her parents had been decorating the girls' room, Catherine had been sleeping on the trundle bed in Jeff's room. She was grateful to Jeff for getting her through the evening, but now, as she lay in bed, she couldn't get to sleep.

"Cath, Cath . . . , are you awake?"

"Yes I am, what do you want?"

"I can't sleep."

Jeff sounded very, very alone. Catherine understood his loneliness because she shared it. "Get in with me, Jeff." He snuggled in beside her, and as soon as she heard the regular rhythm of his breathing, she knew something about herself that Laura had known all along, that she loved her little brother.

Sleep still didn't come to her. Thoughts of Miss Vertue's visit and the events of the evening were pushed to the back of her mind. Now she thought only of Laura—that she might die, never come home, never see them again.

Jeff stirred. Catherine lay rigid beside him. Another thought crowded into her head. Laura was going to die, and her mother and father knew it. Otherwise, why would they be redecorating the room? It was perfectly suited to a wheel-chair the way it was. So why would they be getting a rug? They knew as well as Catherine that rugs get caught in wheel-chairs! Her dad knew that Laura used the hanging-basket chair for her exercises . . . . Now he had taken it down. So they did know. They knew Laura was going to die, and were keeping themselves busy making it a room for one . . . . They couldn't even wait!

Catherine could not bear to think of it another instant. She knew what she had to do. She eased herself carefully out of bed, so as not to disturb Jeff. She stole down the stairs and down the hall into the bedroom not yet finished, turned on the light, opened the can of paint marked 'White' and, dipping a narrow brush into the can, wrote in large letters across the yellow wall the name, LAURA. She put the lid on the can, rested the brush on top of it, turned out the light, shut the bedroom door and stole back into bed beside Jeff. She closed her eyes and immediately fell asleep.

✳ ✳ ✳ ✳ ✳

The next thing she knew, something was shaking her. She groaned and turned but the motion persisted. She felt a hand gripping her shoulder, and as she fought to go back to sleep she heard a voice calling her name: "Kate, Kate, we've good news for you. Wake up!" Her father's voice cut through the weight of her slumber.

Catherine roused herself from a sleeping to a stark-upright position. Jeff was sitting at the end of the bed rubbing his eyes.

"What is it?" she asked, as a chill passed through her.

"Catherine, Jeff, we had to wake you up. We have good news for you. Laura's fever has broken! She is out of the oxygen tent. She is going to be all right!"

Catherine let the words turn round and round in her head. Finally she whispered, "She is going to be all right? Are you sure?"

"Yes, dear, we are sure," Mrs. Devon's voice cracked. Catherine saw her mother was crying. She hugged her mother quietly.

"It's all right, Kate. Both of you can go back to sleep and pleasant dreams. Tomorrow, Laura can talk to you on the phone. Hopefully she'll be home in just a few days."

"We'll have a good talk in the morning," said Mr. Devon. "It's been a long day and a long night. We all need sleep; good night, kids."

He turned out the light and quietly closed the door.

✳ ✳ ✳ ✳ ✳

Catherine had awakened to snatches of humming coming from the kitchen directly below Jeff's bedroom. Those were sounds she hadn't heard since Laura had been hospitalized. For the first time in what seemed to Catherine to have been a very long time, mirth accompanied the conversation at breakfast. Mr. and Mrs. Devon recounted how

Laura's fever had suddenly dipped; how she had talked to them; how she had even asked the doctor if she could talk to Catherine and Jeff on the phone; and how the doctor had said it was possible. It was not until Catherine was told Laura would probably be home within the week that she remembered her deed of the previous night. The sudden recollection of it prevented her responding to her mother.

"When you go to school on Monday, would you have Laura's teachers make a list of assignments? She'll have some catching-up to do." She waited for a response: "Did you hear me?"

"Oh yes, Mom, I will. May I please be excused?" She was already leaving. Maybe, she thought, what she had done had been a bad dream. If it wasn't a dream, obviously her parents hadn't seen the room. She walked quickly down the hall and opened the bedroom door. On the wide expanse of freshly painted wall, in big white letters was printed her sister's name, LAURA.

She sat down as she recalled last night's events—Miss Vertue's visit, her parents' rush to the hospital, her wild suspicions as to why her parents were redecorating the room. She was struggling to collect herself when her father came in.

"Well Kate, now that your sister will be home soon, maybe you'd like to . . . ."He stopped in mid-sentence: "Kate . . . , what is this!" His voice broke: "Kate, did *you* do this? . . . and if you did, *why*?"

"Yes, Dad," Catherine answered softly, "I did it last night . . . . I thought Laura was going to die."

"But why? And that doesn't explain . . . ."

"I wanted to punish you. I thought you and Mom *knew* Laura was going to die, and that's why you were changing the room—to make it a room for me alone."

"How on earth did you get a notion like that?"

"First, Mom told me she wanted me to help her pick a rug . . . . You know as well as I do that wheel-chairs get caught on rugs. Then she blotted out Laura's name on the window sill."

"Catherine, wheel-chairs don't get caught on wall-to-wall carpeting."

"You didn't tell me it was going to be wall-to-wall!"

"You gave us very little chance to tell you anything. Remember, we wanted you to help us, and you refused. Now I think I know why. I wish, Kate, you had talked to us about what was bothering you."

"I don't think I knew all of what was bothering me until last night!"

Catherine's mind jumped to Miss Vertue's visit: "And Dad, I think Miss Vertue *likes* me."

"You didn't know that?"

"No, not until yesterday afternoon when she came to see me. We had a talk on the front porch."

"I didn't know that."

"It was right before you got the call to go to the hospital. I forgot to tell you, because I forgot about it too . . . , until just now. And do you know what? Miss Vertue is nice. She is very nice."

"Oh, Miss Vertue is more than nice. She's kind of like you, Kate. *Nice* is one of the last things you'd call her!"

She laughed. "She helped me understand a lot of stuff I never did before."

"Then I'm very grateful to Miss Vertue."

Catherine thought for a moment before saying, "Dad, there are still some things I don't understand. Why does Laura have to have dystrophy? Why is it Laura who has to be in a wheel-chair?"

"I can't answer that. I don't think anyone can for someone else. If there is an answer for you, it's one you have to find yourself. I do know that Laura has found her answer."

"How do you know that?"

"Because she has accepted her condition. She didn't at first . . . ." His voice trailed off. "She first felt angry, angry that it had happened to her. But she has dealt with that anger and lives every day to its fullest. She doesn't waste her time with either anger or regret."

"Why didn't you and Mom discuss the kind of paralysis Laura has with the two of us? I found out anyway . . . . Pseudohypertrophia."

"Well, you know, Laura *does* know. She has discussed it with both her doctor and with us."

"Then why didn't you tell me?"

"Laura asked us not to. You see, she was afraid that if you knew, you'd treat her differently; that you'd be more mindful of her condition than of her. Your mother and I were not certain that hers was the right decision, but we honored it. Now I think," he said, as he looked at the marred wall, "that all three of us were wrong. I'm afraid, Catherine, we've done damage to your feelings and insulted your intelligence. I'm very sorry."

"No great damage, Dad. But is it true? Will Laura die soon?"

"Who of us *knows* when we are going to die? All we can do is live the best we can for today, *and* for tomorrow."

"I think that that is what Miss Vertue must have been talking about when she spoke of 'Hope.' "

"I suspect you are right."

Catherine broke the silence that had fallen between them. "Isn't it scary for Laura? Until now I've never thought about death. Laura must have been thinking about it for a long time . . . . Dad, it *is* scary."

"I think, when your sister comes home, you should talk to her about it. It would be strange, Catherine, if death felt real to you. You are very far away from it. But for Laura, it is a real thing. I don't believe she is afraid of it."

"Why do you say that?"

"Because she accepted it as something that *happens*. I know that, because I see her preparing herself."

"In what way?"

"Her interest in the past, and particularly those people who were interested in death themselves; Sarah Bernhardt, who had a preoccupation with the subject; Emily Dickinson, who wrote so many beautiful poems about it; then, too, Laura's interest in religion and the various beliefs that are held about life after death."

Her father was right.

"I always thought Laura was peculiar about that, but now I think I understand." Catherine remembered, too, what Laura had said about Aunt Kitty's pin.

This time it was her father who broke the silence: "I am sorry your mother and I went on with the redecorating without your approval. Unfortunately, it's done now, but we should have been more sensitive to your needs."

"No, Dad, *I'm* sorry about the room. I'm sorry I gave you so much trouble. I'm going to repaint the wall this morning."

Her father laughed. "And I'll help!"

"Dad?"

"Yes, Kate?"

"I want to take that piano exam next month."

"I'm glad . . . . Let's go tell your Mom!"

When they walked into the kitchen, Mrs. Devon was on the phone. She handed it to Catherine: "Someone would like to speak with you!"

"Laura, oh Laura, I'm so glad you're better."

Laura laughed a quiet laugh, "So am I, Cath."

"Laura, I thought you were going to die!"

"I am," her sister replied.

"Laura!"

"Well I am," the girl said with a chuckle, "some day. And some day, you will too!"

Catherine smiled, and knew her sister was smiling back. "I've got so much to tell you when you get home."

"I can't wait! They won't let me talk any longer. I'll phone you again this afternoon. Love you."

The phone clicked off.

"There is something I have to ask you, Mother."

"What is it, Catherine?"

"Why did you let Dad take down the hanging-basket chair?"

"Oh dear, I guess you're going to have to tell her, Peter."

"I guess I will. We were trying to surprise you and Laura. We're getting you a record player of your own. We didn't realize our shifting things would raise such suspicions."

"I never could have dreamt that that's what you were planning. Boy, what a neat surprise—a record player! But," she added, still puzzled, "what has that got to do with taking down the hanging-basket chair?"

"We took it from that side of the room because that's where the record player will go. The hanging-basket chair will go on the other side of the window. And this time, I hope I'll find the beam on the first try!"

"Don't worry, Dad. I don't think we could get to sleep without three peacock feathers on the ceiling."

Her mother hugged her tightly, drew her dad and Jeff into the circle and said, "Now I think it's all right to have a cry!"

COLOPHON

This book was designed by Chas. S. Politz
of Design Council, Inc., set in
Compugraphic 10 point Palatino Roman
by Metro-Portland Typesetting,
lithographed on Carnival Offset Ivory
stock by Durham & Downey, Inc. and
case bound with Kingston Natural Finish
cloth by Vintage Bookcrafters,
all of Portland, Oregon.